Who Will Be My Teacher This Year?

Jerry Pallotta

SCHOLASTIC INC.

New York   Toronto   London   Auckland
Sydney   Mexico City   New Delhi   Hong Kong

David Biedrzycki

Thank you to teachers—Martha Harney, Cathy Barker,
Lisa Lawrence, and Laura Anderson.

— J.P.

To my Roosevelt Elementary School teachers, who never resembled any of
these crazy characters. You were all wild and wonderful.

— D.B.

ISBN 978-0-545-33624-6

Text copyright © 2012 by Jerry Pallotta
Illustrations copyright © 2012 by David Biedrzycki

12 11 10 9 8 7 6 5 4 3 2   12 13 14 15 16 17/0

Printed in Singapore   46
First printing, September 2012

I am moving up to a new grade.

I wonder who will be my teacher this year.

I hope it's someone interesting.

A kangaroo could be my teacher.

I'll hop right into learning.

Do I want a penguin for a teacher?

No, the classroom would be too cold.

A moose could be my teacher!

We would have a place to hang our coats.

Do I want a rhinoceros for a teacher?

Yes! We'll charge into reading.

A longhorn would be a nice teacher.

He would be great at moving desks around.

Do I want a jaguar as my teacher?

I heard they give too much homework.

I could have an ostrich for a teacher.

Would he let us outside for recess?

A king cobra could not be our teacher.

The principal said, "No fangs allowed in the building!"

I wouldn't mind a walrus for a teacher.

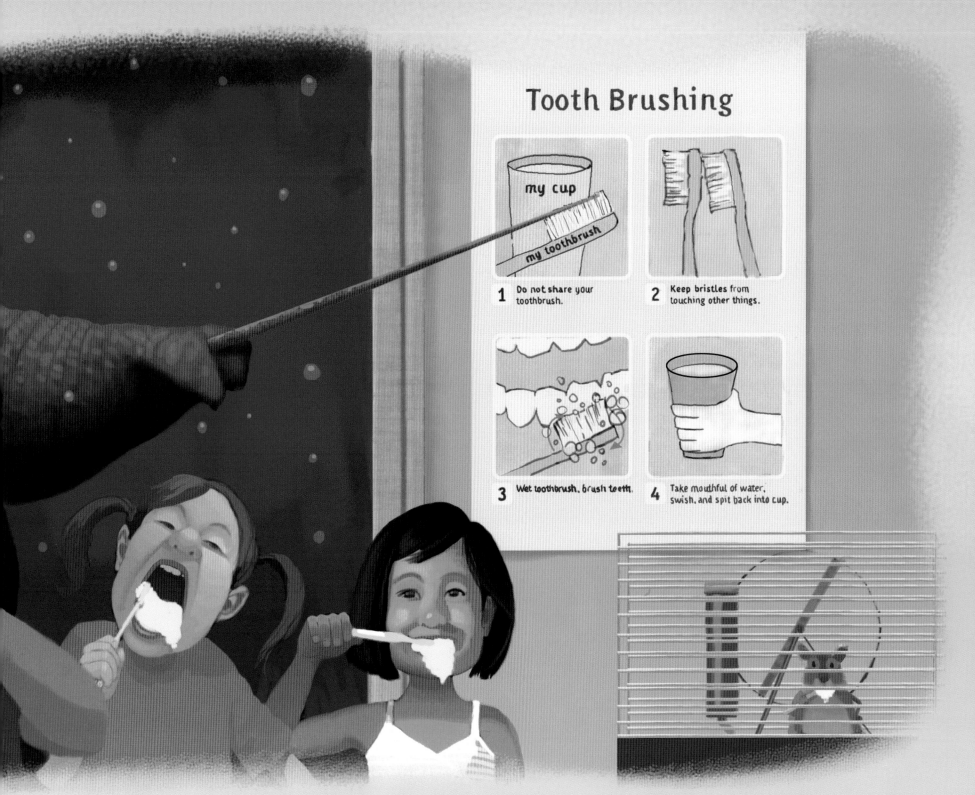

He would teach us to brush our teeth.

A zebra would be an awesome teacher.

She would teach me the proper way to dress.

A pack of wolves would be good teachers.

Math, science, and reading –
we'll get it covered.

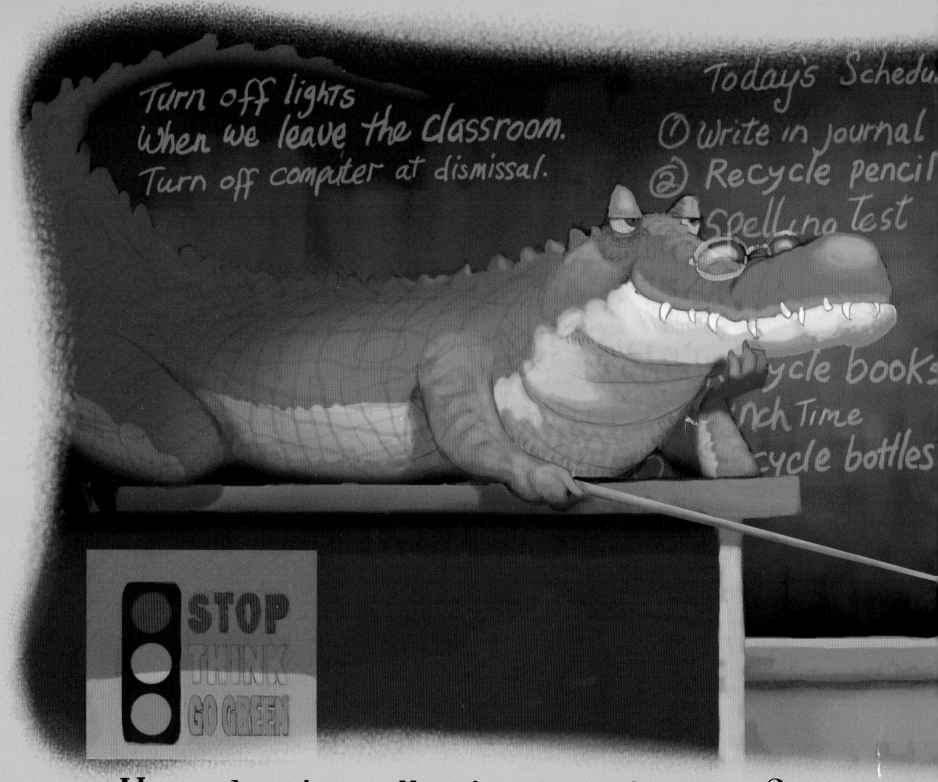

How about an alligator for a teacher?

She could teach us about being green.

Seagull teachers would be way too loud.

I need peace and quiet when I study.

Mom just told me good news –

Ms. Smith will be my teacher. It will be a great year!